101 Manatee Jokes!

Joe Rehfuss

ISBN: 9781520157382

What is the preferred hot beverage of British whales?

Earl Grey manatea

What do you call undersea sporting enthusiasts?

fanatees

how do fish unlock
their houses?

With their manakeys

What is the top mobile carrier under the sea?

manatee mobile

What is really grinding the gears of Old Man Sole these days?

Manateens

What is the top
dessert in the ocean?

Flanatee

Before the big game against Starfish U, what did the Seahorse College coach stress?

manateamwork
Meanwhile, in the Starfish U locker room, their coach kept repeating "There is no I in manateam"

What is the top youth sport in the Sargasso Sea?

Manatee ball

Where did the ancient undersea hunters sleep while tracking water buffalo?

manateepees

At her first showcase, the new manatee artist really impressed with her use of colors. The critics were raving: "So vibrant!" "Great brush work!" "Oh the hue, Manatee!"

What is AC/DC's number one hit on the bottom of the sea?

manaTNT

How do Japanese fish prefer their rice?

mansteamed

What does Miss Pacific Ocean where on her head?

a manatiara

What is the most popular item on undersea playgrounds?

manateetertotters

What does Bart Simpson say when submerged?

Don't have a cow, manatee

whats the hardest part of raising a baby eel?

manateething

Fish: why you so mean to me turtle?

Turtle: I'm just manateasing

What is the key to underwater architecture?

cross manabeams

What happens when sea urchins see sad movies?

manatears

What is the national color of the Atlantic ocean?

manateal

what do wet hobos eat?

cans of manabeans

what do fish wear on casual Fridays?

manajeans

where do fish get honey?

manabees

what is the most commonly injured body part in the ocean?

manaknees

who raises kids under the sea?

manateachers

where do urban seals live?

manacities

what do seal kids watch cartoons?

manaTV

where do fish get financial advice?

manaCNBC

what do hip fish say
before they go to bed?

I'm gonna go catch some manazs

who saves cats caught
in seaweed?

firemanatees

what do kids shoot their eyes out with on the seafloor?

mana-BBs

what do frat boys
drink in the ocean?

manabeers

what do you call a
brownnosing sea cow?

an overmanateever

what do you call a
weak seal?

manafeeble

what is the top mobile game under the sea?

Pokemanatee Go

what do you call a
whale who drones on
and on and on and on?

manatenous

whats for dinner in the sea?

manabeef

what sound do trucks make while they back up in the ocean?

manabeeps

what is the best part of Festivus in the Ocean?

the manafeats of
strength

how many wheels are on an undersea tricycle?

manathree

who stole the sunken treasure?

manatheives

what was Benedict Arnold guilty of on the sea floor?

manatreason

what do you watch movies on if your a fish?

a manascreen

what do you call a
group of ships on the
ocean floor?

a manafleet

who rules the sea bed?

the manaqueen

how do you put a seal pup to bed?

by saying 'manasweet manadreams'

What do you call a great ape when it's all wet?

An Orangutanatee

what happens when
you mix pepper and
sea turtles?

they manasneeze

who hosts the news under the sea?

the anchormanatee

what is the best tax haven in the ocean?

the Caymanatee
Islands

what country makes the best seaweed sausages?

Germanatee

what is the stripiest undersea creature?

the manazebra

where does the ocean
get its oxygen?

manatrees

what is the top snack food in the everglades?

manacheetos

who is the FIERCEST undersea creature?

manaBeyonce

who is her husband?

Jay Mana-z

who is currently topping the billboard top 100 in the ocean?

Justin Manatieber

who played the role of Jack in the undersea version of Titanic?

Manateeonardo DiCaprio

what do you call it when you reach a business deal under the sea?

a managreement

if you believe you are wrongly convicted in seaweed court, what are your options?

manappeal

what do parrotfish eat with?

their manabeak

what is the top indie pop duo under the sea?

Manategan and Sara

who is the star of the hit AMC zombie show the swimming dead?

Normanatee Reedus

what do you call really happy seals?

manaelated

what animal builds the best dams in the ocean?

manabeavers

what insects rule the seven seas?

manabeetles

the fastest animal
under the sea?

the manacheetah

what is the smartest
undersea creature?

the chimpanatee

What is the top
musical under the sea?

ManaGrease

What is Radiohead's top hit in the everglades?

manacreep

what did the evangelical pastor call the unconverted?

manaheathens

what undersea holiday usually falls in April?

manaeaster

which part of the face is responsible for hearing?

the manaear

what is the top digital media format for music in the ocean?

manaCDs

what about for films?

manaDVDs

what are most of
these jokes?

a manareach

what is the strongest oceanic metal?

manasteel

where do you go to get married in the ocean?

the manasteeple

how do fish freshen
their breath?

manaspearamint

what is the most vulnerable part of a fish's foot?

the manaheel

how often do dolphins get paid?

every 2 manaweeks

what are the most popular sea cow milk products?

manacheese and ice manacream

what language do first year computer science students learn in the Sargasso Sea?

manaC++

when do fish go golfing?

manatee time

whats on the outside
of sea bananas?

manapeels

who won the academy award for best undersea performance?

the rainmanatee,
Dustin Hhoffmanatee

who ruled Ancient
Undersea Greece?

the manaceasar

what do you call marine mammals from Italy's largest city?

Romanatees

what do you get when you rub a magic lamp in the ocean?

a managenie

who is the strongest
X-man in the ocean?

manaJean Grey

who is the leader of an undersea church?

the manapriest

what do you call a
lady marine mammal?

a manashe

what sound do sheep make when submerged?

a manableat

what club do ambitious, musically inclined undersea students most often join?

the managlee club

who leads the fortune 500 companies based in the ocean?

chairmanatees and manaCEOs

what planet do fish aspire to visit?

manavenus

what is Elton John's biggest undersea hit?

Rocket Manatee

what about Billy Joel?

Piano Manatee

and Mumford and Sons?

Hey Little Lion Manatee

Black Sabbath?

Iron Manatee

and ZZ Top?

Sharp Dressed Manatee

What do you call a traditional Chinese instrument when its all wet?

a dew gong

Made in the USA
Monee, IL
14 August 2020